DORIAN GREYHOUND

DORIAN GREYHOUND

A Dog's Tale

by
Sheryl Longin

Illustrations by
Martha Szabo

ibooks

DISTRIBUTED BY PUBLISHERS GROUP WEST

In memory of Byron, who made the world brighter

An ibooks, inc. Book

Text Copyright © 2005 Sheryl Longin

Art Copyright © Martha Szabo
Cover painting and drawings by Martha Szabo

www.marthaszabo.com

Distributed by Publishers Group West
1700 Fourth Street, Berkeley, CA 94710

ibooks, inc.
24 West 25th Street
New York, NY 10010

The ibooks world wide web site address is:
www.ibooks.net

First ibooks printing September 2005

ISBN: 1-559687-159-8
10 9 8 7 6 5 4 3 2 1

Printed in the USA

DORIAN GREYHOUND

A Dog's Tale

I
In the Name of the Hose

The limitations of the written word prohibit my favored olfactory form of introduction, so I must resort to the banal human practice of offering my name. I am Dorian P. Greyhound, and please, refrain from inquiring about the derivation of the middle initial. If I wished to share this information, I would have done so. In all other areas, I trust you will find me most forthcoming.

Over the years, I have endured countless requests for the story of my life, but denied them all. Suspicions naturally arose that I had something to hide, a skeleton in my closet. (How I wish. Dental problems have recently restricted me to synthetic bones.) The truth is that most memoirs are tedious stuff, and I had no wish to add to the slush pile. The way I perceived it, every tree that was chopped down to make paper for another dreary reminiscence was one less location to lift my leg.

1

It took a pan of double fudge brownies to make me see the error of my ways. Who left them out uncovered on the kitchen table all night remains a mystery. Should I have known better than to devour them in a midnight frenzy? Of course. Did my sleepwalking excuse pass muster? I do not think so. But after a near fatal allergic reaction to chocolate and an intimate encounter with a stomach pump at the emergency veterinary clinic, I began to rethink my position on leaving something for posterity. Circumstances had left me childless, so if I wished to pass on the wisdom accrued over a lifetime of struggle, I would have to take up the pen. It was a daunting task, given my lack of fingers, much less opposable thumbs, but I had overcome far greater challenges.

The humbleness of my origins never fails to surprise even those who know me well. On occasion, my strict sense of decorum has led to accusations of snobbery which I hope to put to rest with this account. Armchair psychologists have suggested that my adherence to etiquette has been a form of compensation for my mean and brutish rearing, an attempt to show the world that at least I was not raised by wolves.

In fact, my upbringing was in some ways far crueler. Before we were yet old enough to form memories of our mother, all five of my litter were torn from our furry Madonna's side and taken away, never to see her again. As for our sire...to this day I do not know if he was ever made aware of our existence. But save your tears, for we were hardy pups, too filled with the friskiness of youth to feel sorry for ourselves.

The sun was shining, the wind blowing against our faces through the open rear window of the battered station wagon in which we were rolling around, and some delicious smells were wafting toward us from the front seat. I shall never forget the one spot of kindness that was shown to us on that journey from home, when the driver tossed back a handful of blissfully oily yellow sticks (yes, that is how unschooled I was). Oh, what were these salty, soggy morsels from heaven, and would I ever taste more? (Alas, I have recently been restricted to what is sardonically named the "heart-friendly" diet. I try not to whimper when the errant french fry is unwittingly dangled before my dripping nose.)

Much more of the fateful ride I do not remember. The view through the dusty window revealed an endless desert panorama spotted with brownish scrub brush and tumbleweed. Each time we hit an especially jolting pothole, one or the other of my more delicate brethren would release the partially digested contents of their stomachs so that it soon became difficult to find a dry patch on which to lie. That familiar sweet stench lulled me to sleep and even today, whenever I smell it, I am filled with longing for my lost brothers and sisters.

I awoke in the clutches of a large calloused hand which yanked me from the wagon and tossed me carelessly to the ground with the other pups. Before we could untangle ourselves, we were blasted with a stream of bone-chilling water. The hose. I would experience its brutal icy force all too frequently in the coming months. Coarse laughter rang out from the wielder of this diabolical instrument as we huddled together, shivering and shaking our sodden coats.

"Little stinkin' furballs. The puke party's over." It was a voice I would get to know far too well over the next two years, loud and boorish as the man himself. Filled with dread, I looked up into the face of my worst nightmare: Wayne Billy Larry Buttklapper.

Reflecting back on those days from my cushy upholstered daybed, it seems unthinkable that I spent my formative years under the bulbous thumb of this vulgarian. What combination of luck, perseverance and good breeding was responsible for my journey from wretchedness to the moisturized feet of My Beloved Mistress? I have asked myself this question over and over, but I always seem to end up licking a particularly vexing spot at the base of my tail which knocks all rational thought right out of my head.

Tearing my gaze away from the frightful Buttklapper, I surveyed my new surroundings with no small measure of despair. Two rusted trailers were parked next to a barbed wire pen. Adjacent to that was a gated chain link fence which wrapped around a small cracked patch of concrete. No grass or trees or even a growth of weeds sprung from the gravelly dirt. A rough, two-lane highway was visible in the distance.

I was just finishing this cursory inspection when I heard the sound of an engine sputtering to life. I snapped my head around to see the old station wagon that had delivered us to this ghastly site stirring up a cloud of dust as it sped off toward the highway. I watched as it disappeared on the horizon, carrying with it my faint hope for one more french fry.

CLANG! The door slammed shut on my cramped abode. It had been several months since my siblings and I were unceremoniously enrolled in Buttklapper's School For Fast Dogs. We were here to be shaped into track hounds, racing dogs that would "bring in the dough," Buttklapper bellowed at us daily. For a long time we puzzled over what this meant. What use was dough without an oven? And how would running around in a circle inside a barbed wire fence, chasing a dirty stuffed white rabbit glued to a long pole help us to acquire any?

Buttklapper's instructional methods were, shall we say, less than inspiring. Barbaric is the adjective that springs to mind. Also unsound. And nonsensical and counterproductive and odious. We spent our days and nights in solitary confinement, one creature per flea-infested crate. There was barely enough room for us to stand with bowed heads and if we twisted our long bodies into semi-circles, we were just able to turn around from front to back. Seven days a week, in the pitch black before dawn, we were rudely yanked from our cages (and whatever comforting dreams in which we sought shelter) and forced outside in the frigid night air to relieve ourselves on a barren slab of asphalt which was immediately hosed down. Before we'd had an opportunity for even one little sniff! Buttklapper's mercilessness knew no bounds. Then we were given a few sips of brackish water and sent into "The Ring."

For the next few hours, as the fiery Arizona sun scorched its way onto the horizon, Wayne Billy Larry Buttklapper tried to turn us into racing dogs. At least I assume that was his intention. Either that or he simply enjoyed screaming at the top of his lungs and chasing us with a leather whip until he collapsed in a sweaty heap on a plastic chair, swilled a six pack of foul smelling lager and fell into a deep snore-wracked slumber. When he awoke in mid-afternoon, he would shovel a pile of unspeakable slop into a dirty trough and invite us to "dig in." Then we were thrown back in our cages so the leaden mass could settle in our distended bellies.

Until the sun went down, Wayne Billy Larry would retire to his own dank quarters in the adjacent trailer. What he did in there every afternoon has thankfully remained a mystery. All I do know is that it involved gargantuan amounts of bacon, the grease from which he used to moisten our daily rations. At night, the hellish cycle would begin all over again. Another round of training in "The Ring," this time with the tattered rabbit. Apparently, we were supposed to covet this mangled ball of fluff. Why, I cannot imagine. But Buttklapper dangled it in front of us every night. And every night we would stare at it apathetically, while he became increasingly apoplectic.

How long this continued, I cannot be sure. Days and weeks and months blended into one another, each as dreadfully boring as its predecessors. Our puppyish flat faces metamorphosed into elegant, elongated snouts. In spite of the swill we were fed, our limbs grew strong and sinewy. One afternoon, Buttklapper awoke from his second nap of the day and stared at us with surprising intensity.

"Time ta earn yer keep, ya lousy freeloaders." He belched loudly and staggered into his trailer. We looked at one another apprehensively. Something was expected of us. Something to do with the rabbit, no doubt. As oily clouds of bacon smoke blotted out the sun, we pondered our unknown future.

It was only a matter of days before we were facing it head on. After a hair-raising ride in Buttklapper's newly acquired salvaged hearse (not an auspicious vehicle), we arrived at a vast concrete arena which somehow managed to look inconsequential despite its monumental size. As he led us around the back, Buttklapper inhaled deeply. "Smells like money!" he cried out giddily. I beg to differ. The place was crawling with people, all of whom bore the same glassy-eyed expressions and sweaty faces as Buttklapper (a look I was too naïve to recognize as that of the compulsive gambler).

I shall never forget the moment I first laid eyes on the dog who would change my life. He was raising a leg as he faced the crowd, waiting for his umpteenth blue ribbon. Señor Foxtrot was an outsize beast with an ego to match. I could not have wished for a more suitable mentor. That he deigned to notice me, a green young bumpkin without an ounce of experience, was something of a scandal at the time, especially among the more seasoned track hounds whose company he scorned. Perhaps, in my jaunty bearing, he recognized something of his youthful self. Either that or he just liked the way I smelled. Regardless, his interest in me propelled the other racers into fits of jealousy which did little to ease my abrupt transition into the sporting world.

After he emerged from his customary liver-scented Jacuzzi bath and Swedish massage, Señor Foxtrot summoned me for an audience. Not one to beat around the bush (preferring instead to sniff it, then leave his mark), his advice to me was concise and crystal clear: "Keep your eye on the rabbit and run for your life." There was so much more I wanted to ask, but I dared not overstay my welcome. It was time for his pedicure and from the way he was gingerly licking his left forepaw, I garnered it would be quite painful.

The next thing I knew, Buttklapper was rounding up his wards and herding us toward a low standing, gated enclosure. Inside, we found ourselves the only fresh faces in a sea of battle-scarred veterans. My siblings were positively vibrating with fear. I tried to comfort them as best I could, but the truth was I had no more idea what was about to happen to us than they did. And the old timers appeared less than forthcoming. Soon enough, we were prodded into tiny cubicles and the entrances were slammed shut, leaving each of us alone in the dark. I heard one of my sisters whimper. Poor dear! I clawed at my prison walls, desperate to rescue her.

Whoosh! Daylight flooded in as the front of the cubicle was lifted. Before I could take a breath...BANG!! A gunshot ripped through the air. I leapt blindly from my box, my eyes adjusting to the glare, and there it was, looming in front of me—the Rabbit. True, it was only mechanical, but the sun made the white paint on its back shimmer temptingly nonetheless.

Lest I give the impression that track owners are a squeamish lot, I hasten to point out that altruistic concerns do not figure prominently in the decision to use an artificial lure. Unlike its flesh and blood counterpart, the metal bunny is low maintenance and reusable. No muss, no fuss and easy on the pocketbook.

Keep your eye on the rabbit and run for your life. Señor Foxtrot's sage words rang in my ears. I took off, heart pounding, limbs slicing through the heavy air. Around me I heard the roar of the crowd, the crunch of paws hitting gravel. The bunny. The bunny. She was getting closer. Faster! Faster! I was almost there...

BOOM! It was over. She was gone! Where? What happened? My chest was heaving as I panted for air. Suddenly, a hand grabbed me from behind, yanking a leash over my head. It was Buttklapper, his usual foul expression replaced with an even fouler one. "Loser." The word oozed from his lips in a low hiss. Out of the corner of my eye I glimpsed the smirks on the faces of my peers as Buttklapper dragged me off the course. I heard the mocking asides. "There's an opening at the tortoise track." "What's your name, Molasses?" But my shame was overshadowed by a puzzling observation. Why was Buttklapper leading only me away? Where were my sisters and brothers? I swallowed my pride and begged an answer from one of my canine taunters.

Abruptly, the derision stopped, replaced with a grim silence. Every single hound on the track was staring at me with a terrifying combination of shock and pity. "Please," I implored. "Tell me!"

Not one of them, with all their ribbons and trophies, had the courage to speak. I dug my claws into the dirt. The rope around my neck went taut and I gasped for air while Buttklapper tried in vain to make me budge. "What happened to them?" I sputtered. Finally, a tough-looking black and brindle with a half-bitten ear stepped forward. "They didn't even know how to stay on the track. They were... disqualified." I shook my head dumbly. "Disqualified? But where are they?" He did not answer, but his silence spoke volumes.

Keep your eye on the rabbit and run for your life. Señor Foxtrot's message echoed dully in my head. I let out a howl of anguish.

That first night back at Buttklapper's School for Fast Dogs was the loneliest of my life. Wind rocked the trailer causing the empty cages to rattle hauntingly. The smell of my lost siblings pervaded the room, and I kept waking from fitful slumber thinking they were still beside me. Each time reality hit me, I felt as though a knife was being plunged into my heart. By the time Buttklapper hurled me into the pre-dawn, gloom-shrouded Ring, I had steeled myself against any thoughts of the past. My memories provided nothing but soul-weakening sorrow.

As Buttklapper began his customary tirade, it quickly became apparent that, in spite of my determination to persevere and yes, win (not for him certainly, but as a vindication for my lost family), the brutal oaf's lack of coaching experience doomed me to failure. That I had managed to complete my freshman race at all was just short of a miracle; my innate athleticism would carry me only so far.

I spent the morning absorbing his mindless abuse, but as soon as he reached his most agreeable condition of comatose inebriation, I curled up in a ball and pondered my options. To remain under his tutelage was to ensure my eventual demise. I had no illusions about the fate of "losers" in this cutthroat sport. Perhaps there were kinder caretakers than Buttklapper (at least my remaining traces of optimism let me imagine the possibility), but I knew he would sooner let me starve than forgo one slab of his precious bacon. According to his mercenary philosophy, I was meant to be his meal ticket, not vice versa.

Clearly, my only hope was to escape. As quickly as possible. I did not concern myself with future plans. The unknown could scarcely be worse than my current prospects. I glanced over at Buttklapper. His head had flopped sideways and a viscous stream of saliva was flowing out of the corner of his mouth. With each gurgling snore, the coarse black hairs which protruded from his nostrils were sucked back in by the suction force of his inhalation. An earthquake and ten fire engine sirens would not rouse him.

I crept to the edge of the barbed wire fence and started to dig. The dirt was packed so hard it was like clawing at cement. Slowly it gave way beneath my insistent paws. I needed just enough of a depression to wriggle beneath the wire. With one eye cocked toward Buttklapper, I pummeled the earth until my paws were bleeding and foam spewed from my muzzle. Just a little deeper... That's it!

I shimmied into the hole and slipped under the fence. As I emerged on the other side, a barbed wire spike snagged my fur and ripped through the tender skin of my back. Searing pain shot down my spine, but I clenched my teeth to avoid yelping. I could feel warm droplets of blood trickling down my coat. Without looking back, I sprang up and took off toward the highway. I needed no rabbit to lure me; I was running for my life.

The merciless sun beat down on me as I lay in a lifeless heap on the side of the road. Who knows how long I had been here? I remembered trudging through several blazing days and shivering through as many nights without a scrap of nourishment, my parched tongue yearning for water. Whenever a car appeared on the horizon, I laid low, fearing discovery by Buttklapper who, truth be told, was most likely glad to be rid of me. Flies gathered on my dirty, raw wound. Dehydration began playing tricks with my mind. There was my mother, wagging her tail in welcome! I sped up my pace. And right behind her, holding a meaty pig's knuckle between his dazzling teeth...Señor

Foxtrot! But no. As I approached, they melted into the asphalt—mirages. Suddenly, my legs buckled with exhaustion and I collapsed into an inviting oblivion.

It was the sound of a car door slamming which roused me from my delirium. My eyes were crusted over with sand, so I could not see whose strong hands lifted me from my nearly final resting place and carried me back to the vehicle. I felt a soft blanket beneath my withered haunches as the hands gently placed me inside. Something wet touched my mouth. I lapped greedily as blessed water was squirted into my mouth. Then the door slammed again, more footsteps, another door, the rattle of keys, the low rumble of the engine, and we were moving. I let my head sink back on the blanket, too weary to care where I was headed. I was alive.

II
A Moveable Beast

As I lay in the back of this life-saving vehicle transporting me to parts unknown, I had just three concerns: food, liquid refreshment, and a hot bath. Well, perhaps not the last item (I confess a dislike of water except in beverage form). But the hurried opening of all windows, followed by a heavy-handed dispersion of lemon scented air freshener suggested this was of pressing importance to my rescuer. Even in my diminished capacity, I realized that I was breathtakingly malodorous and in desperate need of a vigorous scrubbing. What I was entirely unprepared for was the extent to which my entire body, including its most private orifices, would soon be lathered, rinsed and probed. I am referring most specifically to that sensitive region, until then a veritable No Man's Land—the teeth and gums.

After some hours on the road, I felt the car slow and then come to a complete stop. Those same gentle hands reached in and lifted me out. Although my eyelids remained sealed with dried mud, I experienced a strange and for me altogether new sense of security as I was carried inside. Judging from the resulting gasps, my appearance was yet more distressing than my smell. Almost immediately, I was laid on a cold metal surface, and a damp cloth graciously wiped across my eyes.

It took a while for my vision to come into focus, whereupon I found myself to be in an unnaturally hygienic facility with glaring white walls and a number of stocky, short-haired women wearing pastel smocks. I craned my neck to see the face of my savior who remained steadfastly at my side. The azure blue eyes set deeply in that weather-beaten visage looked down on me with such unexpected kindness that my tail began uncontrollably rotating in fast little circles. In hindsight, this was a rather unfortunate reaction, since it led to the unseemly moniker Loopy with which I was now stuck for the foreseeable future. "Atta boy, Loopy. You're a feisty fellow, ain'tcha?"

Who was this red-haired stranger with poor grammar that had taken pity on a heap of skin and bones lying by the side of the road? I did not have long to ponder that question before a sharp prick on my right flank stole my attention. One of those pastel-smocked women was sticking something long and sharp into my leg! And Big Red, as I decided to call him, wasn't lifting a finger to stop them. I started to struggle but suddenly my body refused to comply; my limbs felt frozen and lifeless. I looked up forlornly at the smiling stranger. Could it be I had let my congenital optimism deceive me? Was this creature I had imagined my savior in truth a conscienceless opportunist? With my last ounce of energy, I turned my head away in silent rebuke as blackness washed over me.

If there is one thing I loathe, it is braggadocio. My ability for self-scrutiny is, dare I say it, a rare trait in my species (let us be honest, in all species). It is with that in mind that I feel honor bound to reveal a debilitating imperfection suffered by most of my breed. Greyhounds have bad teeth. There, the cat is out of the bag. Contrary to popular belief, it is not our fault. We dutifully gnaw at the same leaden and abrasive packaged dog treats whose labels tout their teeth cleaning virtues as every other domestic canine. We do not indulge in sugary between-meal snacks. Many of us even suffer the indignity of having our teeth brushed daily by a zealous master. The paste may be a delicious liver flavor, but do not mistake our excessive salivation for enjoyment. I can safely speak for all greyhounds when I say that dental work of any kind is a traumatic ordeal. Although I was mercifully sedated that day, my first experience under the drill proved no exception.

I awoke with a dazzling new smile and a mouth so sore I feared I would never be able to lick myself again. But my tribulations were far from over. More of those infernal injections were soon in coming. Distemper, rabies, the positively gothic sounding heartworm, to name but a few. I acknowledge the world is a filthy place, full of unsavory parasites and invasive microbes, and I am grateful for the advances of modern medicine which allow me to sniff fellow canines' deposits freely, without fear of contagion, and yet I cannot help but feel that nine (I repeat, nine) inoculations is excessive.

The endless poking and prodding combined with the cloying scent of cheap cologne that I had been doused with (after getting an admittedly gratifying brushing from one of those charmless short-haired attendants) to inflict upon me a most diabolic headache. I was convalescing in an airy cage, gingerly sipping some tepid water when the red-haired stranger walked in, each clomp of his cowboy boots sending a shockwave through my aching skull. And yet...one look into those sparkling blue eyes and my pain and disappointment melted away. His smile hit me like a ray of sunshine, and it was not merely the light bouncing off his gold front tooth. I would follow this man anywhere. "Hey good lookin', you ready to blow this popsicle stand?" My ears pricked up, my breath came in eager bursts; I had absolutely no idea what he was talking about.

For an underprivileged youth such as myself, travel had only been by insufferable means to a dismal destination. I shall forever be indebted to Big Red not only for saving my life, but, as significantly, for introducing me to the joys of the open road. Only the tender ministrations of a loving owner can surpass the sheer heaven of a rolled down rear window and the anticipation of thrillingly foreign scents at each highway rest stop.

Like me, my auburn hero traveled light. I do not recall him changing his clothes at all on our journey (except for a new T-shirt after a messy incident involving a pothole and a double chili cheeseburger). We were footloose and fancy free and we liked it that way (though my subsequent discovery of the greater bliss of domesticity, along with certain remorseful remarks he uttered in his sleep, made me wonder, in retrospect, if my rootless friend was a wanderer by choice).

I prayed these happy-go-lucky days would last forever, just me and my fellow traveler roaming the by-ways, stopping to smell the flowers (or in my case, muskier attractions), catching forty winks in the backseat of his old Firebird parked overnight in the lot of a well-lit convenience store. To be sure, the elusive metallic bunny still haunted my dreams, taunting me to catch it, then suddenly morphing into a scowling Buttklapper who lunged for me. Mercifully, that is when I would awake, whimpering, and seek comfort by burying my nose in the pile of unwashed socks Big Red thoughtfully tossed into the rear footwell as my improvised mattress.

The last day of my extended idyll dawned like all the others, with a security guard banging on the window and ordering us to remove our vehicle from the premises or face the iron clamp of a police impound truck. After a hurried breakfast of kibble and jelly donuts (oh, sweet memory! Woe be it, they have joined the ever-lengthening list of forbidden fruits after My Beloved Mistress adopted a household ban on refined sugar), we burned rubber out of the latest nameless town and headed toward the cloudless blue horizon. I had no inkling of what was to come. Big Red made sure of that. He was not one for prolonged goodbyes.

It was not callousness which led him to hand me over to a total stranger with nothing more than a "See ya', Loopy," before jumping back in his home on wheels and disappearing from my life forever. No, I understood all too well that he suffered from an excess of emotion. The stack of crisp green bills he quickly pocketed, and my discovery only hours later that half the dogs at "The Ranch" were delivered by him in exactly the same fashion did nothing to quell my certainty that our bond was unique. His tears would be shed in seclusion, as would mine.

"Bones" is not the name one hopes to hear when being informed of one's new roommate. Quite frankly, the entire concept of sharing intimate quarters with another canine was an unexpected and wholly uncongenial development. I admit that said quarters were substantially more spacious and accommodating than this cage-dweller had been accustomed to. I was ushered into an indoor/outdoor suite, consisting of one room with three wooden walls and a fourth of screen, connected with a roomy enclosed backyard via an ingenious construct—a torso-sized cut-out near the bottom of the wall covered by a loose flap of canvas through which I was able to pass at will (to my mind, the "doggie door" remains the single greatest invention of the previous century). Sweet smelling fresh straw covered the floor of the interior, which was furnished with a large, curious looking object covered in a dingy floral print fabric.

My bitter upbringing led me to view anything new and unidentifiable with deep trepidation. I kept my distance from this unknown quantity, circling it warily. The lanky blonde woman who had brought me inside began to laugh. "Bones! Get in here and show the greenhorn how to make like a couch potato." She reached down and patted my flank reassuringly. "Don't worry, Loopy. This is going to rock your world." She had a big heart, if a depressingly cliched vocabulary, and I was starting to feel comforted, when a streak of white passed through the canvas flap, soared across the room and landed effortlessly atop the mysterious item.

He was a greasy looking scoundrel, with a jaundiced tinge to his pale coat and darting, uncharacteristically beady eyes for a greyhound. I prayed we would not be left alone together. Apparently, my discomfort was not palpable. "Scooch over, Bones. Time to cuddle with your new roomie."

I resisted mightily, but eventually found myself nestled up against the unsavory character who oozed malevolence. I do not recall having ever been more ill at ease. And yet, I had never felt more comfortable in my entire life! My whole body was enveloped in a cushiony embrace. What was this delirious sensation? My head lolled back; my tongue hung slackly from the side of my mouth; I writhed in delight. "Knock yourselves out, fellas." The door banged shut and we were alone.

The next thing I knew, a paw shot out and knocked me hard to the ground. "The couch is mine." Bones was glaring down at me with such cold fury, I felt a shiver run through my frame. It would be lunacy to attempt to reason with him. But the couch...I had only just been introduced to its joys. And now to be deprived of them so cruelly. The couch. The couch. It beckoned to me. It was irresistible. Its allure was driving me mad.

Somehow, I resisted the impulse to leap back up and challenge the petty tyrant. A cooler head would serve me well if I ever hoped to return to that enchanted perch. For the remainder of the day, I managed to stay out of Bones' way while keeping him constantly in my sights. He made it clear that I was not the first roommate to enjoy the pleasure of his company and he left little question about the sorry fate of previous unwelcome houseguests.

I had no doubt I would survive our forced companionship (my mettle had been tested by far worse), but my sights were set much higher than mere survival. If I could convince the beast that I was the most harmonious, unobtrusive, non-competitive creature he ever hoped to meet, he might conclude that getting rid of me would scarcely be in his self-interest. My replacement would end up being more problematic. That realization would give me some leverage in the relationship, which I intended to use to secure my place...on the couch.

I set to it immediately, straddling the fine line between flattery and bootlicking (my own paws offer my tongue enough of a workout). If only I had been less diligent, but that is not my way. My plan worked magnificently, and I had no one but myself to blame for the unforeseen consequences. Bones didn't just decide to tolerate me, he became frighteningly attached. I suppose I should have anticipated that an unwanted, emotionally deprived animal would stand no chance against the onslaught of my estimable charms. I gained access to the couch easily enough. The problem was getting off of it.

Bones' ardor was unflagging. He would not let me out of his sight. He wanted me on that puffy pedestal at all times, with him beside me. At first, I was more than happy to oblige.

This was where I had dreamt of being, after all. In my new-found haven, I slipped into a dangerous laxity, and failed to notice the warning signs of Bones' growing obsession. One day, he became overwrought when I eschewed a piece of rawhide he lovingly proffered. The following day he turned sullen and suspicious after I chose to relieve myself in a fresh spot of clover rather than against the trunk of our usual sycamore tree.

Still, I was unprepared for the eruption of emotional vitriol, which spewed forth about a week later during one of our daily "free-range" sessions. Every afternoon, all the current residents of the Ranch were let out of their "apartments" to run wild over the entire grounds until dinnertime. It was an exhilarating and therapeutic experience for creatures accustomed only to cages, and I tried to make the most of it, never knowing when this privilege might be taken away. The sights and smells of freedom were so new to me, I did not mind being "dogged" by Bones the entire time. In fact, the sensory overload kept me relatively oblivious to my fellow hounds.

On this particular outing, while following the path of a fluttering tangerine-colored butterfly, I suddenly felt a curious tingling in my nostrils. Nose to the ground, all thoughts of butterflies swiftly vanquished, I had to find the source of this intoxicating aroma. A few wrong turns later, and there it was, a fine spray of glistening yellow drops clinging to some recently trampled blades of grass. I inhaled deeply, savoring the complex notes of rose petals, cinnamon, and vinegar. Whoever had left this marking was most assuredly someone I wanted to know.

All at once, Bones was at my throat. A snarling, growling fleaball without an ounce of self-control, he had succumbed to an irrational jealous rage. I knew fighting back would only further convince him he was right, so I rolled over and played dead (a trick I had learned from Big Red who was adept at avoiding bar fights). After a few vicious scratches failed to provoke a response, Bones switched to a verbal attack. The epithets came hard and fast. Colorful though they were, they all amounted to the same thing. I was a treacherous, ungrateful betrayer, and I would pay the price. It seemed futile to point out that I had merely been sniffing around.

His notion of justice was swift and unforgiving. If he could not possess me, then no one would. At first, I did not fully comprehend the implications of my sentence. Bones remained aloof and banished me from the couch, but I could live with that. In fact, it was a relief to be free of his smothering neediness. When I awoke one morning to find him shredding the cushions of the couch in precisely the spot where I had formerly lay, I assumed it was an act of simple malice designed to erase me from his life and send a message that my exile was permanent. How naïve I was.

That very afternoon, as I lay dozing in a corner, the door of our shelter opened and in walked a fastidious looking family of four accompanied by our ranch proprietress. Their admiring glances reassured me that, contrary to Bones' repeated insults, I had not lost my looks. "I know you're in the market for a brindle and Loopy here is our newest arrival. Handsome as all get out and a gentleman to boot. If he was human, I wouldn't be letting him go so easily."

I casually arranged myself in the crowd-pleasing sphinx pose and displayed my most soulful expression. They were appealing, in a wholesome, slightly dull way, and if I played my cards right, they could be my ticket out of the frigid bondage of cohabitation with Bones. The matriarch of the brood wasted no time in determining my suitability. She marched right over, pulled a fabric swatch from her industrial sized shoulder tote, and held it up to my coat. "It's a match. Even if he does shed, it'll blend right in with the new upholstery. We'll take him."

No sooner were the words out of her mouth than Bones let out a fiendish howl. All eyes swerved to find him lying on his relatively pristine side of the accursed couch, staring accusingly at my former end, which was hideously disfigured with claw marks. As if in slow motion, I watched the appalled reactions on the faces of my "could-have-been" adopters, who automatically assumed I was the perpetrator of this vile defacement. I leapt to my feet and rushed over to them, trying to nuzzle my way back into their good graces, but I knew it was useless. They stared at me coldly and left without so much as a pat on the head.

The ghastly smile on Bones' mug spoke a thousand words. His insidious plan had triumphed. There was no way out for me; he would make sure of that. As a final gesture of his dominance, he invited me back on the couch. Let there be no mistake, the invitation implied, it was his to allow me on.

What happened next is not something I am proud of, but this time it was I who lost control. In a flash, the whole of my short, sorry life overwhelmed me. I had endured too much to let things turn out in such an insufferable manner. The last thing I remember was a burst of crimson blooming like a flower and blotting out my vision as I hurled across the room at my surprised nemesis.

I awoke, swathed in bandages, in a sunny, blessedly private cubicle. Once I had determined my senses were intact, I gingerly stood up, relieved to discover my injuries, though extensive, were strictly cosmetic. The lady of the ranch soon appeared and I steeled myself for the worst, whatever that might be. Surely, she would waste no more time on a lost cause like me, a known couch shredder with a violent temper. I dared not imagine what would become of me once I was evicted from this haven for homeless hounds. Still, I held my head high as she approached, and looked her squarely in the eye, prepared to accept my fate. What a fortuitous decision that turned out to be.

"Thank heavens that nasty boy Bones hasn't broken your spirit...because I've found you a home!" Excitement, relief, exhaustion washed over me. I felt my knees buckle and I sunk to the floor. My fairy godmother stood over me, smiling knowingly. "Bones has had six roommates...and six couches. Guess you really can't teach an old dog new tricks." She winked and tossed me a biscuit. As I pondered my suddenly bright future, the cookie's mealy blandness tasted (just this once, mind you) like ambrosia.

III
The House of Girth

First impressions may prove misleading but they are difficult to overcome, so I was naturally quite worried about my scrawny, bandaged appearance the day my adoptive family was scheduled to arrive at the Ranch. They were, I had been informed, sleek urbanites from a glamorous coastal metropolis. As eager as I was to begin life anew, how I wished the lady of the ranch had allowed me another week of recuperation, so that I might look more presentable. Inner beauty is a fine and noble thing, and I was certain mine would be revealed to them over time, but they hailed from a notoriously shallow and image-conscious city. Their initial disappointment in me would be inevitable. Surely they would not possess a couch so distressed it would match my haggard aspect.

Remarkably, I turned out to be wrong on both accounts. As I lay fretting, that fateful morning, atop an old towel, I heard a voice so captivating, I was immediately and fully in its thrall. The possessor of that marvelous instrument drew closer and I dared let myself hope that she was the one I had been waiting for. It seemed like an eternity until the door to my room opened. I tried to restrain myself for fear my neediness would repel her, but it was no use. I could no sooner contain my intrinsic positivism than I could walk upright (perish the thought).

Before I knew what I was doing, I found myself nuzzling a denim-clad thigh, an impossibly tender hand stroking my trembling back. And then she was kneeling down, cupping my head in both hands. Our eyes met and I felt the last vestiges of doubt melt away. She was the one, the answer to my prayers, the reason for my existence. I would cross the oceans, brave the deserts, follow her to the ends of the earth...My Beloved Mistress! In a move so bold it still makes me blush, I thrust my neck forward and touched my moist snout to her lips.

"I thought greyhounds were more reserved." I leapt back, startled, at the sudden intrusion of a masculine yet thoughtful voice. Yes, of course, the lady of the ranch had spoken of a couple. Anxiety flooded back over me. Had I overstepped my bounds just now? Would I be rejected in favor of a less

impulsive animal? The very thought of another dog basking in the warmth of my inamorata was too much for me to
bear. I rushed up to the man and threw myself at his feet.
With a wink, he bent down and rubbed my side. "I know just
how you feel. She has the same effect on me."

I prefer not to dwell on the insultingly minimal amount
of paperwork involved in my adoption. Suffice it to say that
if I derived my self-worth from the monetary value placed
upon me, my tail would be permanently fused between my
legs. Besides, as I learned on the car ride to my new home,
I was chosen for a much more compelling reason than my
bargain basement price. I can never fully convey the swell-
ing of pride I felt upon discovering I belong to a (highly
coveted by many pet owners) "hypo-allergenic" breed. This
tag qualifies me for ownership by the most sensitive of all
humans, those whose nasal passages react to substances
undetectable to lesser mortals. Naturally, My Beloved Mistress is a member of this elite corps. Such is the delicacy
of her constitution, that she has difficulty simply drawing
breath anywhere in the remote vicinity of that common
neighborhood scourge, the domestic feline. Other canines
are equally problematic, as well as certain plants and grass-
es. I pity them all, deprived of the joys of her company.

The first half of the journey from the Ranch to my permanent abode passed by in a blur. Close proximity to My
Beloved Mistress kept my heart pounding and my senses
trained on her, although I do recall being puzzled by the
source of an intoxicating aroma emanating from the smooth
and slippery seats (this being my first encounter with the

enticingly treacherous leather upholstery). The Master exhibited a sure hand behind the wheel and a mellifluous singing voice (which helped to camouflage the sound of my embarrassingly heavy panting). For the first time in my hardscrabble existence, I was traveling in style.

I am confident they would have gotten to it eventually, but I feel certain my decorous behavior in their luxury automobile focused my new guardians' attention on the ludicrous inaccuracy of my Ranch appellation. "Loopy," My Beloved Mistress's lovely lips curled in disdain, "sounds like a reject from the seven dwarves." "Or a deranged circus clown," added my master. "Aren't they all?" The Adored One replied. Thus ensued my first exposure to their typically wry banter. Clever potential names were tossed about, then rejected as being unworthy of yours truly. Giving credit where it is due, I acknowledge it was not My Beloved Mistress who came up with the winning selection, but her erudite partner who first uttered the words "Dorian Greyhound." For that, he was rewarded with a kiss and I was instantly reborn as the dog I am today and forever.

Mere words cannot convey the splendor that awaited me curbside at my new address. I refer not only to the wondrous cacophony of scents (many no doubt left as calling cards from my canine neighbors) but also to the inviting terra cotta wall which fronted the property. Its rich patina would only benefit from years of legs raised against it. To indicate my pleasure, I christened it immediately, a gesture greatly appreciated by my new family, judging from the lavish praise which followed. "What a good boy, Dorian!

That's right, do your business outside! Good Dorian! Good Dorian!" How I loved the sound of that name. Each time it was spoken, my ears perked up proudly, invoking even more praise and more name-calling. "Look at that, I think he already knows his name! Good boy, Dorian! What a good, smart Dorian!" Unaccustomed as I was to such effusiveness, I felt a rush of warmth filling me up and raised my leg against the wall again. My Beloved Mistress grinned. "Have I got a middle initial for you? Dorian P. Greyhound, welcome home." There, the mystery is revealed.

Thank heavens for the unconditional emotional support I received from My Beloved Mistress and the master. Without it I would surely have been undone by the unforeseen perils of domestic life. I speak not only of the obvious culprits such as stairs (a canny space-saving invention of mankind which I had to be taught to navigate), sliding glass doors (cleanliness is not a virtue) and swimming pools (if we were meant to immerse ourselves in water, we would have been born with gills, thank you very much), but also of more insidious ones. As I would come to learn, even my fleet metabolism was no match for overflowing bowls of high quality kibble supplemented with tasty morsels prepared in the finest of restaurants and specially packaged for me in "doggie bags," combined with the scrumptious table scraps my loved ones dutifully slipped me under the dining table, not to mention the gourmet dog treats I devoured several times a day.

My cup runneth over and I was lapping it up, encouraged by my well-meaning guardians who were determined I should want for nothing. Between meals and vigorous massages (I was living the life of a Kobe cow) I wiled away the hours on a gloriously lengthy L-shaped couch, the color of sunshine (not for long), with a slight depression at the elbow which made it unfit for sitting but in which my curled torso rested most easily. I received numerous visitors in those first few days, friends and relations of My Beloved Mistress and master, who were eager to make the acquaintance of the newest addition to the family. Although I rarely roused myself from the couch during these meet and greets, I attributed my general feeling of sluggishness to the strain involved in such forced cordiality.

One afternoon, trying to relieve a slight cramp in my foreleg, I strayed from my usual path between couch and kitchen and ventured into a small tiled room that I had noticed was frequented by guests who entered, shut the door and then emerged several minutes later. I had idly speculated on what drew them in, but was unprepared for the shocking surprise that lay in store. Inside, all I observed was a sink and a large, low porcelain bowl attached to a tank with a handle on it. Curiouser and curiouser. I sniffed around, but the room had recently been sprayed with a cloying floral air freshener which overpowered any natural aromas I might have discerned. I was about to give up and wet my whistle at my water bowl, when I saw something that nearly made me jump out of my skin.

There, standing right before me was another greyhound with perhaps the most beautiful brindle coat I had ever laid eyes on, and a serious weight problem. A spare tire of flesh hung from his once muscular, now paunchy torso. He stared back at me, apparently as stunned by my presence as I was by his. For several moments neither of us moved, and when we did it was in exact synchronicity. I felt sorry for the poor fellow and vowed I would never let myself go to seed like he had.

I took a step closer, the better to get a good whiff, and so did he. As I stretched my neck towards him, my head hit something hard. I jumped back. He did the same. We looked at one another in confusion, then tried again. Some invisible barrier was keeping us apart. We both began barking in consternation. "Dorian, what's the matter?" My Beloved Mistress called out from the living room. I ran out to get her and led her back into the little room where my compatriot waited. As he and I resumed barking, My Beloved Mistress burst out laughing. "Oh my darling dog, you've never seen a mirror, have you?" Patiently, she led me right up to him, then tapped against the reflection. "See how handsome you are, Dorian?" I stared at my image in disbelief. No, it could not be! What had happened to my athletic physique? I hung my head and whimpered like a puppy.

After several tasty treats which My Beloved Mistress forced upon me to soothe me and which it would have been impolite to refuse, I made a resolution. Gluttony and sloth were pleasures I could no longer afford. Did I not owe it to My Beloved Mistress to become the best greyhound I could be? If that meant forgoing the leftover sushi and dry-aged T-bones, so be it. To test my newfound resolve, I spent the dinner hour camped at the feet of My Beloved Mistress, studiously ignoring each succulent morsel of free-range chicken skin slipped to me under the table. At daybreak of the following morning, I leapt from my couch and, instead of loitering noisily around my food bowl in hopes of rousing my keepers to breakfast, I prepared to tackle my greatest challenge... the stairs.

For a creature with a cruising speed of forty-five miles per hour, the inability to master something as elementary as graduated steps was deeply humiliating. So far, I had feigned indifference to the attractions of a glass-walled loft accessible only by a steep and narrow staircase (but with views to send a sighthound's pulse racing). In truth, I was desperate to venture up, but lacked the fortitude to brave the towering obstacle. Now, something stronger than fear took hold of me. The stairs offered me salvation, a way to have my cake (and rib-eye and smoked salmon and scrambled eggs with caviar) and eat it too. The stairs, if mastered, were a home gym for canines. As I stood at the bottom, looking up at the steep incline, I could already feel the burn in my quadriceps. I closed my eyes and visualized myself racing up and down, sure-footed, muscles pumping, excess poundage melting away.

With a deep breath and a flurry of butterflies in my stomach, I took the first step, then another. So far, so good. This was not terribly difficult after all. A few more and I was feeling quite full of myself. Certain I made a fine sight poised halfway up and eager to show off my new prowess, I let vanity get the better of me and did something so downright stupid I still shake my head in dismay. I stopped. Front legs on one step, back legs several steps below, I let out a loud bark to alert My Beloved Mistress, then waited as she inevitably came running. Hearing her gasp of admiration, I compounded my fateful error by craning my neck and turning to look down at her (the operative word being "down").

To those who have never been struck with the sudden disorientation of vertigo, I say count your blessings. I consider it a bona fide miracle that my house-breaking training held as I clung to the stairs, paralyzed, so dizzy I was incapable of lifting a paw. My Beloved Mistress rushed up and tried coaxing me gently towards the landing, but I was rooted to the spot, and at my current weight, far too heavy for her to budge. With the supreme presence of mind she always exhibits in moments of crisis, she sat down calmly beside me and stroking my back, began to "talk me up" with promises of belly rubs and fleecy chew toys. Gradually, the spinning slowed down until it had ceased completely and I was moving again with My Beloved Mistress's words of encouragement filling my ears. The next thing I knew I was at the top and she was making good on the first promise.

The return trip, although comparatively smooth sailing, was not without its own form of challenge. Determined to avoid the mistake of my freshman ascent, I took off at an accelerated clip. There would be no stopping on the way down. What I had failed to consider was the momentum I would gather, regardless of starting speed, as I descended. By mid-point, I was hurling downwards at an alarming, ever-increasing velocity. The wall opposite the bottom of the stairs loomed dangerously close. My ability to stop on a dime was dubious under optimal conditions, but the well-waxed wooden floor awaiting my thundering paws ensured maximum slippage. I steeled myself as best I could for the unavoidable crash and prayed mine would be the only nose out of joint when it was all over.

A round of applause from My Beloved Mistress did much to mask the pain of a bruised snout as did her jocular pronouncement of the entire expedition as a "smashing success." I would be lying if I said I turned right around and marched triumphantly back up, but within a matter of days I was well on the way to solo mastery. By month's end, I was as nimble as a mountain goat, with thigh muscles so well-defined they tempted My Beloved Mistress to clad me in bicycle shorts for Halloween.

Truly, now, I had reached a state of utter contentment. I lacked for nothing, physically, emotionally or materially. I had a sturdy red-tiled roof over my head, a strong mind and body, and the love of a good woman (and man). My Beloved Mistress constantly (while scratching my ears) asked what more she could do for me. Each time I remained silent, at a loss for words. How the days and weeks and months flew by, until, before we knew it, it was our one year anniversary. When My Beloved Mistress and master presented me with a monogrammed leather collar, I was overcome with sentiment and, unable, because of my large stature, to crawl into her lap, instead laid my head adoringly there. Oh Nirvana! It was a pose we slipped into daily which, although I did not know it at the time, would provide my most cherished and painful memories in the months to come.

The first hint of clouds on the horizon came during one of My Beloved Mistress's scintillating and scrumptious dinner parties. I was a frequent visitor to the table during these events, politely making the rounds to mingle with each guest, yet never overstaying my welcome. If I came away with a few choice morsels, so be it, but it was never my intention to beg. In fact, many a household canine would be well advised to follow my lead. My irreproachable etiquette (above all, no whimpering) frequently redounded to my advantage with bountiful handouts from appreciative diners.

I believe it was near the end of the cheese course (a terrifically moldy Spanish blue and a raw French ewe's milk with a mouth watering stench reminiscent of a young boy's unlaundered gym uniform) that an unusually callow acquaintance of My Beloved Mistress and master raised his glass of after dinner spirits and toasted their impending adventure. My ears instantly perked up and I looked over inquiringly at the one I adore. She smiled back, but not before a flicker of unease passed across her radiant visage. I quickly moved around the table and slipped my head under her outstretched hand. "Will you be renting out the house?" the impertinent fellow asked. My heart began pounding in my chest. "And what are you going to do about the dog?" With that, I darted out of the room, hoping My Beloved Mistress would not notice my distress. She had spent hours preparing this feast and I was determined that my anxiety would not dampen the success of her efforts.

I should have known better than to think her watchful eye would miss my frantic departure, anymore than I might have overlooked hers, bound together as we were by an un-breakable empathic connection. Minutes later, as I lay forlorn-ly atop her brand new cashmere dressing gown which I had snatched off her bed in a sudden fit of pique, she appeared in the doorway and shook her head contritely. "I'm sorry, Dorian. I should have told you right away. But I couldn't bear it."

So it was true. I buried my head in the plush folds of her robe which she ever so gently pulled out from beneath me as she kneeled down and stroked my hairless pink belly. "Think of it as a lovely vacation. You'll get a chance to be with anoth-er dog. It will be good for you." For the first time in our idyllic relationship, My Beloved Mistress was dissembling. We both knew that being apart from one another would be nothing short of hell on earth.

A groan of utter woe emerged from the depths of my soul. My Beloved Mistress lay her head down next to me and whispered into my ear with a quavering voice. "I'll be back as soon as I can and then I'll never leave you again." I extended my paw across the elegant robe which now rested firmly in her grasp. She looked at me in surprise. "Most dogs settle for a dirty T-shirt as a reminder of their owner." I rested my head back on the robe, all the while looking at her. A stream of tears was rolling down her fair cheeks. "Promise you won't forget me, Dorian P. Greyhound?" As if that was possible. As if I had not memorized every detail of each moment I had been graced with her presence in order to protect myself against just such an unthinkable calamity. She curled up next to me, pulling the robe over both of us, and I felt her body wracked with sobs.

IV
Valley of the Dogs

Undoubtedly, it was with my best interests at heart that My Beloved Mistress and master made the unusual choice of placing me, for the sultry months of July, August and September, in an un-air conditioned tract home in a desert-like suburb while they worked abroad (in a foreign country that had, according to them, a rather cavalier attitude towards the ethical treatment of animals). There were other options. "Doggie spas" or "canine retreats" advertised luxe accommodations for the family pet, and professional pet-sitters (who moved into the home to spare the domesticated creature the emotional upheaval of moving out) were a dime a dozen in a city populated almost exclusively by aspiring thespians and personal fitness trainers. If My Beloved Mistress had determined one of these alternatives best for me, I am certain she would not have balked at the exorbitant rates for a ninety day stay at the Bed and Biscuit

Inn or at the prospect of a nineteen year old self-described "frat-boy type" rooming without adult supervision in her exquisitely decorated hillside hacienda.

To characterize my state of mind on that searing morning when I was deposited at my summer residence as depressed would be a significant understatement. Granted, My Beloved Mistress's uncontrollable sobbing did little to encourage stoicism, but it was no excuse for my disgraceful "accident" on my foster family's living room carpet. That they seemed unperturbed should have been a warning sign to me of the general laxity of the household, but grief had temporarily dulled my acute observational skills.

The departure of My Beloved Mistress remains to this day so harrowing a memory that I dare not explore it in any detail. Had it not been for the loud rumblings emanating from my stomach at the approach of dinner hour, I might very well have remained in my fugue state indefinitely. So it was over a bowl of soggy kibble that I first came face to face (and what a face it was) with my constant companion for the season: Brittany, an English Bull Dog several months my junior (the jowls suggested otherwise, but one never questions a lady about her age).

As pellets of dog food flew past my head (not, I hasten to point out, a reflection of poor manners, but rather an unavoidable consequence of her unfortunate underbite), I thanked her for graciously sharing her humble repast and promised to remain as unobtrusive a houseguest as possible. Dipping my head down to clear the floor of stray morsels, I was unprepared for the enthusiasm of Brittany's response. A warm bubble of saliva encompassed my head as the sturdy creature threw herself at me in a welcoming embrace.

Although I have spent the better part of my life in predominantly human company and it is with humans that I have enjoyed the most rewarding personal relationships, I remain cognizant of the fact that I am, first and foremost, a dog. As such, I naturally assumed I possessed an innate understanding of canine behavior, in all its forms. My cohabitation with Brittany was about to disabuse me of this erroneous presupposition. In truth, my knowledge of my species was limited almost exclusively to the peculiarly uncharacteristic behavior of my own breed.

Fetching, hoarding, burying, and (most perplexing of all) mindlessly chasing cars—the allure of these activities was inexplicable to me. Brittany, bless her heart, could frolic for hours with a dead tennis ball and a mound of fresh dirt, her frantic digging periodically interrupted by a spontaneous burst of barking at nothing at all. The crater-filled moonscape of the backyard reflected her preoccupation with this pastime, in which she never ceased entreating me to participate. It would have been rude of me to abstain, so on several occasions, I gave it the old college try. Despite my best efforts, I was unable to find anything to recommend it. A furtive peak through the fence into adjacent lawn-damaged yards revealed I was alone among neighborhood dogs in my lack of interest.

Perhaps a more disciplined mind than mine would have taken advantage of the lack of mental stimulation to embark on a rigorous exploration of the self. And while I admit to a talent for prolonged idleness, the prospect of an endless summer with no distractions challenged my capacity to avoid boredom. This, coupled with my relentless pining for My Beloved Mistress, made me fear for my very sanity. Only some sort of unconscious self-protective brain mechanism to ward off madness can explain the sudden interest I began taking in Brittany's "affairs of the heart."

During the first weeks of my stay, I went out of my way to ensure that, despite our shared living space, Brittany's privacy remained inviolate. If my zealousness in this regard was interpreted as aloofness, I regret the misunderstanding, but not the good manners from which it resulted. Brittany's self-esteem issues were unknown to me at the time.

I could not, however, fail to notice the dramatic change in Brittany's laissez-faire attitude towards her personal appearance each time a certain local scalawag came nosing around the side gate. He was hardly a paragon of cleanliness himself, with his matted fur and perpetually mud caked paws, so it struck me as perhaps counterproductive for Brittany to focus on grooming as a way to attract him. Still, I kept these thoughts to myself, not wanting to discourage any efforts on her part to make cosmetic improvements, whatever the motivation.

While I will stop short of calling him a stray, the fellow stretched the limits of domestication. Since our infrequent walks with my sedentary human hosts never extended beyond the cul-de-sac at the end of the street, I was never able to verify his vague claim of living "around the corner." He did sport an untarnished registration tag on his otherwise grimy collar, so I had no reason to believe he was not up-to-date on his shots. Whether he was a victim of careless masters, or intentionally affected the "abandoned" look, the result was the same. The fairer sex were drawn to him like (and in addition to) flies.

Sweet Brittany's devotion to this scoundrel was boundless and, as far as I could tell, completely unreciprocated. To be fair, he did call at our gate on a regular basis, but only as one stop on his rounds of the neighborhood. Thankfully, the wrought iron bars prevented him from getting too familiar, for Brittany lacked the willpower to resist him and I fear he was no gentleman. A couple of sniffs, a few sweet nothings murmured in her ear and she was ready to share the thirty-pound kibble bag with a complete stranger.

Although it pained me to watch Brittany delude herself with fanciful visions of white-picket fences and doghouses built for two, I held my tongue. After all, who was I to force bitter reality down her throat? Did I not rely on dreams of a reunion with My Beloved Mistress to sustain me? Brittany had a right to her own fantasies, however foolish they seemed to others. Her giddy rolls in the grass and the tail chasing that preceded each visit from her faithless "beau" harmed no one.

I make no claims to psychic gifts, but I did awake with a feeling of foreboding the morning the tree trimmers were scheduled to prune the overburdened carob trees in my hosts'"rustic"patio. Although the layers of shriveled brown pods littering the property suggested the trees had been ignored for years, it was not until a visiting elderly relative, while bending over to examine a large mushroom growing out of the base of the tree, was struck on the posterior by a heavy and sharp-cornered falling pod and threatened legal action, that the occupants appreciated the necessity of occasional yard work.

The valiant garden workers cannot be held responsible for the events that succeeded their visit. That this overburdened duo managed to remove the detritus of a decade's neglect in ninety-degree heat without so much as a water break was astounding. Their failure to securely latch the gate before rushing to an even more arduous job across the street is hardly worth mentioning, and would have gone unnoticed, if not for an ill-timed visit from our local shaggy reprobate.

To Brittany's delight, the clearing of the backyard had exposed a plethora of hidden treasures, ranging from the typical mangled teddy bear to a mummified salamander to quite a few vintage unopened school report cards. Preoccupied with her newly-discovered booty, she somehow missed the usual predatory growls that signaled the arrival of her rebel without a cause. Factoring in the element of surprise and her already euphoric mood, it was inevitable that she would throw herself at the gate in her haste to nuzzle the dripping snout protruding through the bars. I would like to believe that, with prior knowledge of the open latch, she would have tried to hold herself in check, but such idle speculation is moot. Unwittingly or not, she pushed the gate ajar. The consequences were undeservedly harsh, regardless of her culpability.

The hours Brittany had whiled away, dreaming about what would happen in the event of such an opportunity, in no way prepared her for the reality of the situation. Having passed through the gate, she stood, momentarily paralyzed, on the threshold of the unknown. Should she throw caution to the wind and follow her heart and her Prince Charming (ever the opportunist, he wasted no time in snatching up a half-masticated pig's ear suddenly accessible to him through the open gate) even if it meant abandoning the only home she had ever known for an uncertain future?

In the blink of an eye she was gone. I blinked again, just to double check. No sign of either of them. To be perfectly honest, I was hardly concerned at first. I assumed that after the first blush wore off, in ten minutes or so, Brittany would come bounding back, with a renewed appreciation for the status quo. I did briefly consider taking advantage of the temporary escape route to make my way across town and back to My Beloved Mistress' vacant hillside aerie. One glance overhead at the fiery midday sun convinced me otherwise. Who was I kidding? My days of roaming the desert were long past. Besides, good breeding prevented me from disappearing without so much as a goodbye to my warm-hearted friend.

Anticipating her imminent return, I decided to feign slumber so she could sneak back in unscrutinized by prying eyes. Did I mention the fiery midday sun? Several hours later, I was mortified to discover that Brittany was not the only dog in residence who drooled in its sleep, and equally distressing, the young damsel was still in absentia.

Gathering my wits about me, I removed the blades of grass encrusted on the side of my muzzle and ran through a list of possible explanations for her failure to come home. It was a short list, but unanimously grim. The feeling of foreboding with which I had awoken that morning was now settling over me like a dark cloud. Or so I thought, until a sudden clap of thunder, followed by a burst of rain alerted me to the arrival of a rare summer storm.

As I ran for shelter under the overhang of the home's roof, it occurred to me that the downpour would soon cause Brittany's masters to wonder why she had not retreated indoors. Perhaps it would be for the best if they discovered she was missing and mounted an all-out search for her whereabouts. Yet I still harbored hope she would return on her own, avoiding the humiliating short leash treatment she would otherwise incur.

I paced anxiously beneath the eaves, waiting for the inevitable calls ("Brittany! Come! Watch those muddy paws!"). Sure enough, within moments of the first drops I could hear them fruitlessly scouring the house for her. Then, just as I predicted, footsteps made their way toward the back door. My heart sank as I had to acknowledge she was not going to manage this clandestine rendezvous. The doorknob started to turn and I held my breath, waiting for the humans, when amazingly,

Brittany came skulking into the yard. Her tail was between her legs and she looked like a drowned rat, but no matter.

"Quick! Grab that dried up lizard. Pretend you have been playing with it." She looked at me, confused, but a lifetime of obedience training paid off, and she hurriedly followed my admittedly nauseating orders. Just in the nick of time, I might add, as the back door opened and a head poked out. "Here she is, honey!" The master of the house yelled inside. "She's soaking wet and she's got something putrid between her teeth." "I told you we should have gotten a poodle," came the female response from within. "At least they've got something going on upstairs."

After the grand disillusionment she had just experienced, her mistress's insulting words rolled off Brittany's back like beads of water. She dropped the soggy reptile and trotted dutifully inside, murmuring her gratitude as she passed. I nodded and followed her in, and that was the last we spoke of the whole sorry incident. It was apparent from her demeanor that things had not turned out well, but I admired the stiff upper lip she developed as a result. (It had the added benefit of somewhat restricting half-masticated kibble from spilling out of her mouth at meal times.)

Truthfully, I found this new subdued Brittany a more congenial comrade. Though I regretted that her sudden maturity had been gained through emotional suffering, I also knew, from my own experience, that valuable life lessons were rarely learned any other way. Her villainous ex's decision to permanently steer a wide berth around our gate was an unexpected felicity. I briefly entertained the notion that he actually possessed an ounce of decency, but Brittany's fearsome snarl each time he was within earshot provided a more convincing explanation for his behavior.

The days were becoming shorter and summer's heat marginally less oppressive when the first inkling of trouble surfaced. I was feeling invigorated by the cooler temperature, so it struck me as odd that Brittany seemed to be lapsing into torpor. In the beginning I attributed her lethargy to the last traces of melancholy being purged from her psyche. If only the root cause had been psychological. Soon enough a telltale symptom emerged. Brittany began to scratch.

Who knows how long she fought the urge, ashamed to reveal her condition? Eventually, the itching became intolerable and she succumbed, clandestinely at first. She would disappear behind a large reclining chair and let loose with her teeth and claws, in a futile attempt to extinguish the infernal sensation. After several days of this secretive behavior, inflamed raw patches became visible on the skin behind her ears and beneath her tail. My fears were confirmed. Brittany had fleas.

If there is a tactful way to raise the subject of parasitic infestation, I remain in the dark about it. Though it chagrined me to do so, I pointed out to Brittany that the hairless red areas all over her body were a dead giveaway as to the nature of her disorder and that, furthermore, she could no longer hide the problem from the master and mistress of the house. Quite frankly, I was surprised they had failed to notice her condition already, but as I mentioned previously, they were prone to laxity.

Brittany's reaction to my remarks surprised me. Rather than taking affront, she expressed enormous relief that I had exposed her secret. She recognized that acknowledgement of her problem was the first step towards treatment (for which she was desperately eager.) The only thing holding her back, she confessed, was fear of punishment by her master and mistress. Since I had never observed any physical cruelty on the part of this rather oafish pair, I believed her trepidation was unfounded; but her ailing condition made it impossible for me to assuage her anxiety.

Some may consider my subsequent actions heroic, but I insist that to do anything else would have been uncouth. For several months, this magnanimous individual had opened her home and her heart to me, sharing everything without reservation. I would never be able to fully repay her countless kindnesses, but an opportunity was now presenting itself to make a small contribution.

Brittany had mistakenly attributed my lack of interest in (her favored diversion of) burying things to a disinclination towards digging. Her amazement was palpable as she watched me suddenly dash outside and begin frenziedly clawing at the dirt in front of the gate. I could not waste time explaining my plan to Brittany, who might have tried to dissuade me, but after her initial shock at seeing me dig, she was overcome with the desire to scratch and left me to my mysterious endeavor. With a speed that surprised even me, I had, by mid-afternoon, excavated a small passage to the street.

All that remained was for me to loiter on the street side until the mistress and master returned home from wherever it was they went each weekday (I knew only that they always came back smelling of microwave popcorn and rubber erasers which led me to suspect they were elementary school teachers). As soon as they saw me, I would put on my best hangdog expression and slink back under the gate, caught in the act, it would seem. But the piece de resistance would come when they called me inside to deliver the expected reprimand. I had been studying Brittany's movements carefully, and was convincingly accurate at mimicking her frantic, herky-jerky scratching.

The scheme unfolded seamlessly, with the unwitting Brittany arriving right on cue, at the sound of raised voices. One glance from me pawing myself furiously to Brittany sporting those raw patches and the snookered couple drew the obvious conclusion. I was a no-good escape artist who had contracted the dreaded infestation during my illicit wanderings, then spread the nasty pests to their innocent, irreproachable pooch. I had been counting on their blind faith in their own pet and a desire to place blame elsewhere, and I was not disappointed.

By the time poor addled Brittany comprehended what was happening, I had been visited with the ultimate punishment. No longer would I enjoy the comforts of my hosts' hearth and home. I was, from this moment on, "an outside dog," forced to brave the elements without shelter, day or night, rain or shine. (Honesty compels me to admit that the mean overnight low in September in the San Fernando Valley is a balmy 68 degrees.)

Bless her heart, the mottled fur ball begged me to allow her to set the record straight with her presumptuous caretakers, but I would not yield. How could she ever understand the pleasure I took from seeing how my life had come full circle? It was not so long ago (and yet, a lifetime) that I had been blamed for something else I did not do (the shredding of my very first sofa). At the time, I had been powerless to clear myself and as a result, suffered a heart-breaking (though ultimately fortuitous) loss. Now, after joyous hours basking in the wisdom and love of My Beloved Mistress and master, I had acquired the insight and self-possession to instigate a similar situation for the very opposite aim. I was not powerless to control my fate. On the contrary, I was able to use my power to help another less fortunate than myself.

Sleeping under the stars that first night outdoors, I felt a lightheartedness I had not known since my separation from My Beloved Mistress. When she returned (did I fail to mention that she was due back in three days?) I was sure she would recognize a new serenity in my bearing, so that when "the facts" were presented to her by my hosts, she would see through them to the nobility of my actions. My only regret was that I would not be able to bid a proper adieu to dearest Brittany. My banishment precluded any physical contact between us, so we would have to suffice with a hurried pressing of wet noses against the sliding glass rear door.

Even now, these many years later, I hardly dare relive the moment of my reunion with My Beloved Mistress. So powerful were the emotions, I feared my heart would stop. Perhaps it did, but the violent trembling of my body was enough to start it beating again. When told of my recent nefarious conduct, My Beloved Mistress held her tongue, thanked my hosts and led me out as quickly as possible. Her silence continued all the way to the car, and I began to imagine the unthinkable. Was it possible she actually believed their version of events? I could not bear the thought that she might think poorly of me. I hung my head, afraid to look in her eyes, as I pounced into the back seat.

She leaned in to shut the door and I dared to glance up. What was this? My Beloved Mistress was laughing. "Fleas schmeeze. Your insect repellent doesn't wear off for another month. Tell me the truth, Dorian P. Greyhound. Was that bulldog running around with a bad crowd?" I rubbed my nose against her cheek, as she threw her arms around my neck. "Not that you'd tell, my perfect gentleman."

V
Tender Is the Bite

Memory had not exaggerated the aesthetic charm of My Beloved Mistress's domestic sanctuary. Its vibrantly painted walls radiated the same warmth and tranquility I had pined for since my forced summer holiday. With our cozy threesome together again in these heavenly surroundings, I marveled at my wondrous good fortune, and tried to ignore the little voice reminding me that nothing in this world lasts forever.

My Beloved Mistress had returned from Eastern Europe with a seemingly insatiable appetite for Japanese cuisine. "Sushi deprivation" was the term she coined for her negative reaction to a steady diet of pork with dumplings and cream sauce. (I refrained from pointing out that, had she taken me with her, I would have relieved her of her portion daily, without complaint.) Consequently, she and the master spent their first few weeks home dining out nearly every night at their favorite local sushi bars, and always returning with a piece or two or three for their appreciative chowhound.

So it was with some disappointment but little surprise that I greeted the abrupt finale of this raw fish feeding frenzy. Surely, My Beloved Mistress had satisfied her craving and would resume her normal varied diet. Though I would miss the nightly tidbits from the sea, I looked forward to a cornucopia of doggie bags filled with other ethnic delicacies. How cruel was reality's intercession.

The next morning, I awoke to a sound I had never before heard emanating from My Beloved Mistress's sweet lips. I hope polite company will excuse my failure to find any other means of description, but, in a word, the delicate creature was retching. At first, I was beside myself with fear. What insidious microorganism had maneuvered its way into her unsuspecting digestive system to make its nasty mischief? How long did it plan on staying? Would I be deprived of savory table scraps while the malevolent virus vacationed inside her small intestine?

I hovered anxiously outside the bathroom door, waiting for My Beloved Mistress to emerge and put my mind at ease with an offering from the cookie jar. Time passed slowly, as it always does before breakfast (the pre-dinner hour is even more tedious), and my agitation got the better of me. I began pawing at the door and whimpering most pitifully, until it was opened and a faint voice called me inside. I hasten to add that I would never enter this most private sanctorum unless invited. But I do believe my presence was more of a comfort than an intrusion.

The most fair one was standing at the sink, understandably pale as a shade, and yet...I could scarcely believe my eyes. She was grinning from ear to ear! Oh, that cursed bug. It had affected her vibrant mind, only temporarily I prayed, but nonetheless, I began to tremble. As she reached out to still my quaking head with her tender hand, she serenely uttered the words that would forever alter my existence. "We're expecting a baby."

Of all the sorry behavior I have laid bare in these pages, there is none that shames me more than the ensuing period in my life. I was a selfish cur, an infantile lout, a pathetic ingrate; nay, far worse. What made my attitude so reprehensible was that throughout the months of My Beloved Mistress's pregnancy, I was a master of deception, hiding my poisonous thoughts and posing as the adoring pet they had so generously welcomed into their hearts. Countless were the times I lovingly lay my head against My Beloved Mistress's expanding stomach, all the while harboring hateful inclinations. I scored extra points for my faithful watch over her daily solo swim sessions, since it is common knowledge that I abhor submersion in water more than nature abhors a vacuum.

In my defense, I can only say that my ill will toward the impending arrival was like a mist that never condensed into a cloud. It hung heavily over me, fogging my better judgement, but never forming itself into a course of action. I am, after all, but a simple beast, my meager struggle toward enlightenment notwithstanding. That I had not fully resolved the residual feelings of deprivation caused by my traumatic puppyhood is hardly surprising. Without benefit of professional help, I had traveled a far distance on the road to recovery. But my efforts to heal myself were no match for the shock dealt to my ever-fragile ego by a new addition to the family.

I counted down the months, then weeks, then days, with dread, certain that when presented with her newborn bundle of joy, My Beloved Mistress would be powerless in the throes of motherhood. All the attention she had lavished on me would prove mere practice for the real thing, a human baby. The furry, four-legged creature who worshipped the ground she walked on would be as good as forgotten, relegated to some inconspicuous corner, far from the new center of her existence, the nursery.

Yet even as I wallowed in despair, my allegiance to My Beloved Mistress never wavered. She remained blameless in my eyes, a victim of the biological imperative to perpetuate her species. I was simply an unexpected casualty of that imperative. I was certain she did not know that her love for me would diminish, just as I was certain that it inevitably would. This belief made the last weeks before the birth exquisitely painful. My heart leapt at every glance she directed my way. I savored each stroke of her passing hand. To think that I would soon be forced to watch silently as another received all that had once been mine! May I never know the torture of those days again.

Naturally enough, the moment of truth, when it arrived, was fairly anti-climactic. The state of frenzy into which I had descended the moment My Beloved Mistress departed for the hospital receded just as quickly when she returned home, blessedly unchanged, save for the surprisingly large (My Beloved Mistress being of petite frame) and fragrant infant cradled in her arms. Though I was not instantly overwhelmed with a transformative love for the rosy babe, the loathing I expected to wash over me did not materialize. Instead, I experienced a mild curiosity, enhanced no doubt by the scent which wafted from its tightly swaddled posterior. I moved closer, snout quivering, and My Beloved Mistress obliged me by lowering the armful so I could get a good and proper sniff.

Ahhh, my first diaper, one of life's unexpected pleasures. I shall never forget it, though there would be countless more, with increasingly piquant aromas. Nothing that emitted this wholesome stench could be all bad. My interest piqued, I continued my olfactory examination down the length of the infant's body until I reached its fuzz-covered head. My Beloved Mistress and master betrayed no suspicion that I harbored malevolent thoughts as they allowed me nose to nose with their precious offspring. So innocent it looked, batting its brown eyes and gurgling softly. "Dorian, meet Tess," they both said in unison. I dared not be impolite. I leaned in to give it a perfunctory lick, and the cunning little cherub opened its mouth, spewing out a stream of curdled ambrosia. My Beloved Mistress and master were aghast, fearing my response. Stunned by the deliberateness of the action, not to mention the child's perfect aim, I took a step back. Then I stuck out my tongue and did what any mature, self-respecting creature would do; I licked away every delicious last drop.

I had underestimated the competition, mistaking innocence for helplessness. It would not happen again. As I soon discovered, I was facing a master of manipulation, able to command the entire household, wordlessly, from its crib. It was impossible not to be impressed and I developed a grudging admiration for the diminutive tyrant. I even hoped, through constant scrutiny of its deceptively minimal actions, to acquire some of those mighty communication skills myself. Happily, My Beloved Mistress interpreted my watchfulness as a sign of devotion for which I was lavishly rewarded with the protein of the day.

I try not to dwell on the ways in which the lack of a formal education has hampered my development, but my ignorance of physics is a particular sore spot. I am certain Einstein knows better, but (without benefit of a wristwatch) I have determined that time is fluid. How else to explain a single afternoon stretching out ad infinitum, while whole seasons appear to pass with the wag of a tail? And so it was with the infancy of Tess. Her nine months of incubation were, for me, an eternity of apprehension. Yet, no sooner had she arrived a supine body, than it seemed she was navigating the halls on all fours leaving a trail of devastation in her wake.

At first, I avoided her messy path, not wanting to be held in even small part responsible for the destruction she wreaked. One day an army of ants exposed the short-sightedness of my cowardice. Her tracks turned out to be a mouth-watering goldmine. Owner of an appetite nearly as insatiable as my own, the tiny traveler never ventured anywhere without sustenance, usually smeared liberally over the very same appendages she used to maneuver throughout the house. Imagine my added joy upon discovering that My Beloved Mistress would reward my tireless crumb removal with an additional treat. In fact, my housecleaning efforts were so appreciated that I was promptly called to service each time the bacchanalian child was buckled into her high chair. "Dorian," My Beloved Mistress would cry out, waiting for me to leap into position before steering a spoonful of mush toward its wavering target. "Let the food flinging begin!" I daresay not a single droplet of strained peas eluded my agile tongue which even probed the formidable toe crevasses of a flailing baby foot.

So it was that a visitor to our humble abode would have observed nothing but sweetness and light: a bouncing baby, her doting parents, and their indispensable, unflappable four-legged companion. Surfaces, as we all know, can be deceiving. Only the sheer exhaustion of keeping infant hours (three awake, one asleep, ad "exhaustium"...) prevented my simmering resentments from boiling over. Less fortuitously, it also prevented My Beloved Mistress from giving me my nightly rub down which, now more than ever, I sorely relied upon. I felt my grip on civility loosening. Without opposable thumbs (or even fingers for that matter), it was only a matter of time before I let go completely.

I am not inclined toward superstitious beliefs. Quite

frankly, discussions of the paranormal fatigue me. Rather, I choose to interpret the explosion of a raw sewage pipe beneath our troubled household as a sharp illustration of symbolism. And if no one else was witness to an understandably frazzled baby-sitter flushing the last of three (in one night) non-biodegradable diapers down a toilet, was the diaper ever actually flushed? My lips are sealed.

There is no doubt, however, that the introduction of an unwitting stranger into our tenuous situation could only lead to misfortune. I highlight the hulking wordlessness and Neanderthal brow of the specialist sent to do battle with our wayward plumbing not to justify my subsequent crime, but simply to establish the context in which it was committed. Indeed, I will not whitewash my transgression. It was an offense against man, a violation of the law, and I remain entirely unrepentant!

My words are not intended to shock, though I am certain that will be their effect. I simply must speak the truth or I will be compounding my misdeeds. Imagine a baby blessedly sleeping in a stroller, a Beloved Mistress beside herself with weariness, dozing even as her foot pushes the pram back and forth to maintain the constant rocking motion without which the infant will howl into alertness. From around a corner, a hostile looking alien with multiple blunt and sharp instruments hanging from his substantial waist, makes an unexpected appearance. He is moving purposefully toward the defenseless child. All that lies between them is a prescient canine.

So I leapt. So I bit. I broke flesh. I drew blood. (A wee

drop. Nevertheless...) I did what every cell in my body screamed out for me to do. I protected my loved one. My Loved One. Tess, that unwanted little intruder into my perfect existence...Oh, how I adored her.

In the tumultuous aftermath of my appalling infraction, this conclusion did not immediately present itself. My Beloved Mistress quite properly attended to the victim, isolating me in a remote laundry room to await, she assured him, a thorough reprimand. As she led me to my cell, she loudly berated me (purely for his benefit, I later learned) in an unfamiliar tone of voice that chilled me to the bone. I was relieved when the door closed so that I might be alone with my dishonor. Only then, as I began to reflect on the egregious behavior, was its true import revealed.

The realization of my profound attachment to a human baby entered my consciousness like a lightning bolt. But the joy of this discovery was immediately superceded by a desperate thought. What if the plumber pressed charges? I had only just acknowledged my tender emotions. To be removed from their object, as I would undoubtedly be, was more than I could bear. My misery was aggravated by the memory of time wasted. All those weeks of sulkiness, when I could have been nuzzling the dewy cheeks of my precious darling Tess. How I would miss her mellifluous drooling gurgles, that tiny thumb, perpetually wrinkled from sucking, the omnipresent wet spot she left on My Beloved Mistress's shoulder, and oh, that unlimited supply of crumbs.

I dared not meditate on the fate of a biter in a home

with a small child. Even if My Beloved Mistress and master evinced full confidence in my tameness, I doubted the authorities would concur in light of my troubled upbringing. My near perfect record as an obedient pet could never erase the stigma attached to a "rescue" dog. Questions would be asked and the seeds of uncertainty planted. I, who would risk my life to protect fair Tess, could hardly expect less of her flesh and blood. Their responsibility was clear. I had to be removed. If our roles were reversed, I would do the same.

By the time My Beloved Mistress released me from captivity, I was convinced of my dire future. Despite her assurances that the wounded had a forgiving soul, made even more so by her substantial contribution to his "retirement fund," my instincts told me otherwise. I had tasted the man's blood; it was absent mercy. It was only a matter of time before an investigator from the Department of Animal Control rang our front doorbell to take me away. Though it would be the hardest thing I had ever done, I vowed I would go quietly, determined to spare My Beloved Mistress undue agony. Knowing she had a lifetime with Tess to give her succor was a bittersweet comfort to me, but one I would cling to in whichever penal colony I was incarcerated.

Each day's postal delivery sent me into a fresh panic as I watched My Beloved Mistress shuffle through the thick pile. It was during this period that my aversion to junk mail took root, as my torture was prolonged with every credit card invitation and magazine solicitation. Although I knew my reprieve was only temporary, how I rejoiced when the entire bundle was discarded unopened, proof that no ominous notification had yet arrived.

Were two psyches ever more perfectly aligned than My Beloved Mistress's and mine? Just as I wished to protect her from sorrow by hiding my fear, so she kept secret the impending appointment with the Inspector to shield me from the awful inevitable. Her face betrayed nothing as she perused the mail, so that I awoke on doomsday itself without the slightest inkling of what was to come. In hindsight her wisdom seems obvious. A nervous dog would only confirm the Inspector's suspicions. Still, when I imagine the self-control she exerted, keeping her emotions in check for my sake, I am humbled.

I was scouring the seat cushion of Tess's highchair with my tongue, employing a rapid abrasive movement to remove an unsightly but still flavorsome crust of desiccated broccoli puree, when I heard an unfamiliar automobile pull up outside. By the time a pair of sensibly shod feet marched down the driveway to our door, I was in position on the other side, announcing the visitor's presence in a resonant tone. It is a point of some pride that no doorbell has ever taken me by surprise.

A confidentiality agreement bars me from revealing specifics about the interview that followed. I gather such measures are rare, but mine turned out to be a most exceptional case. Above all, I wish to protect the identity of the very fine Inspector whose superiors might not appreciate the wisdom of her actions in this matter. They would, of course, be wrong, but the Department of Animal Control can ill afford to suffer the loss of a stellar employee.

I can only say that I was scrutinized thoroughly and my comportment tested in a number of stressful situations. Naturally, I passed effortlessly through these psychological tests and the Investigator moved on to the more relevant interview portion of the proceedings. Upon discovering, during routine questioning of My Beloved Mistress, that the victim was a plumber (and not, as her faulty records stated, a refrigerator repair technician), the Inspector became noticeably intrigued. I cannot honestly recall whether she inquired about his name or My Beloved Mistress volunteered the information, but her reaction upon hearing it was startling.

"You broke skin, Dorian?" the Inspector cried out, arousing me from my intentionally submissive pose in the corner. As My Beloved Mistress looked on in utter bewilderment, the delighted woman began rubbing my head with glee. "I only wish I could have been there." I admit that her abrupt display of affection caused me some momentary confusion as well, and even doubt about her soundness of mind, but I decided to take full advantage of her enthusiasm. "That charlatan told me I needed all new copper plumbing, then he ripped apart my kitchen, installed plastic pipes which burst two months later, and sent me a trumped up bill. He'll be seeing me in small claims court."

After some discussion between the two gentlewomen, in which the Inspector actually proposed that I be awarded a Certificate of Merit for my Actions in Defense of the

Public Interest, it was agreed that the case file would be sealed, and my record would remain unblemished. Before she departed, the Inspector treated me to an exceptionally satisfying deep tissue massage, and I felt the tensions of the previous twelve months begin to melt away. What I needed now was rest. I could not remember my last untroubled night of sleep.

As drowsiness overtook me, I found myself gravitating to the one carpeted room in our decorous hacienda. Not for me right now, the chilly tile and distressed hardwood flooring that appealed to the eye but not the limbs. I could have retreated to one of the fleecy "dog beds" thoughtfully installed throughout the house, but I suddenly desired fluffy pink wall-to-wall pile on which to stretch my weary bones.

And so it was that My Beloved Mistress happily discovered me, several hours later, blissfully asleep beneath the crib of My Other Beloved Mistress... My Beloved Tess. Although she feigned amusement at my choice of this draft-free and pleasantly overheated spot as my permanent bedroom, I know my nightly presence in it is a source of great comfort to her and the master. No batteries are required for the new baby monitor.